MW00898659

To:_____

From:_____

Date:_____

Alisa Hope Wagner is an award-winning author of Christian fiction and non-fiction books. She has a red birthmark on her right hand and arm.

You can find her at her blog, www.alisahopewagner.com, and at her Facebook and Twitter: @alisahopewagner. Purchase her books on Amazon.

Albert Morales is an award-winning illustrator of comics, young adult fiction and children's books. He has a dark birthmark on his right hand.

You can contact him at artwise310@hotmail.com and find him on Instagram: @angryroosterstudios and Facebook: @albertmorales

Finding Her Friends
Butterfly Princess Book 2
Marked Writers Publishing
www.markedwriterspublishing.com
www.alisahopewagner.com
Written by Alisa Hope Wagner
Illustrated by Albert Morales
Colored by Bryan Arfel Magnaye
Edited by Patricia Coughlin,
Holly Smith and Daniel Wagner
Formatted by Alisa Hope Wagner
All rights reserved
ISBN: 978-1-7334333-4-1

FINDING HER FRIENDS

Butterfly Princess Book 2

Now that Laia, the Butterfly Princess, was no longer afraid of Swift Swallow, she decided it was time to find true friends. She shyly introduced herself to each butterfly of the meadow, but her sincere requests met with similar ends.

"Tisk, Tisk!" one butterfly shouted. "Your birthmark is too red and bright. A bird, a lizard or even a snake will see us and sneak a bite!"

"You are a risk!" another butterfly spouted. "I don't want to be seen with you. Your wing is so strangely splattered and there's nothing more to do."

Laia returned to the shadows of the forest, friendless and alone. "What use is life in the fair fields," Laia cried, "if I have no friends of my own?"

Finally, she decided to approach Queen Mama and King Papa with her firm request. She wanted to explore the lands beyond their home for friends who suited her best.

King Papa reassured. "We'll miss you, our dear Butterfly Princess, but we know you're alert, brave and smart. We give you our consent on this quest that you're eager to start."

Queen Mama agreed. "And once you find those true friends of yours, please bring them straight to me. I'm happy to welcome them into our tree and serve them my honeyed hibiscus tea."

After hugs and tears and forgetting all fears, Laia soared along the breath of her parents' cheers.

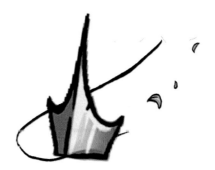

Now, Laia's wings were unusually strong and her flight unquestionably quick, and she zipped down unfamiliar paths faster than lickety-split. She was so intent on soaring away that she didn't notice the brash zooming sounds coming her way.

Suddenly, a grisly, glaring monster—like a moving mountain of mayhem—hissed right past her.

Then another massive mammoth whooshed by. Then another. And another. They sprinted down dark, steamy asphalt with smoke streaming behind the chase. They were brassy and loud with feet made of rubber that spun at an impossible pace.

"What is that awful creature?" She cried. "I don't recognize a single feature! I believe that ugly beast is called a car—a metal monster that comes from afar!"

They disrupted the air around the Butterfly Princess and swept her into a tornado for one. Her lavender wings wobbled and swiveled, and her golden antennas whirled and spun.

She yelped, "Oh no! My friend-finding pursuit is undone!"

Finally, the twister released its daring grip, and she fell down, down into a dry, shrubby strip.

Once her head stopped spinning and her wings disbanded, she fluttered up slowly to spy where she had landed.

Laia was horrified to see lines of menacing monsters roaring on either side. Now she was stuck in the brushy middle with nowhere to go and no place to hide.

"Now I'll never find my true friends," she whined, looking around at the ugly scene. "A pretty spot is where all friendships begin, but everything here is unpleasant and mean."

"This is not so," the Wind did whisper. "Friends can be found in the roughest of shade. Simply look up and down and to and fro and under every grassy blade."

Laia shrugged her shoulders and gave a slight sigh. "Well," she thought, "I guess I could try."

She hopped along the twiggy path and peeped about the ugly land, and she avoided stepping down the dry earth-cracks dusted with sand. Finally, she heard a familiar buzzing sound and spied a young bumblebee sitting on the ground.

He sobbed and blubbered with a buzz, buzz, buzz as teardrops sprinkled down his yellow and black jacket of fuzz.

"Hello," she said, startling the lad. "My name is Laia. What's your name and why are you so sad?"

The young bumblebee wiped his wet cheeks with his waxy arm. "My name is Ben," he said. "I am from a nearby farm. I'm crying because I don't have a single friend. The other bees tease me because my stinger is blunt on the end."

Laia nodded kindly and revealed her fiery flame. "I do believe we are feeling the same. I have a birthmark on my wing. You have a stinger with no sting. Join this adventure with me, so together we can find true friend number three."

So, the two friends began their journey. Laia crept through wispy weeds, and Ben's wings hummed against the breeze.

Suddenly, a green grasshopper popped into view. "I don't mean to pry, but I overheard you talking as I hopped by. My name is Lee, and I was wondering if I could be friend number three."

Laia looked at the friendly grasshopper a bit confused. "No offense," Laia said, cautiously, "but there's nothing different about you."

"Oh, yes, there is!" the grasshopper exclaimed and held up his stringy legs. "Can't you see? There's nothing there. I don't have my pegs."

"Why is that wrong?" Ben, the bumblebee, buzzed.

The grasshopper looked very sad. "Without my pegs, I can't play a song."

Laia smiled. "Lee, you will be our true friend number three. Now, let's a explore, so we can find friend number four!"

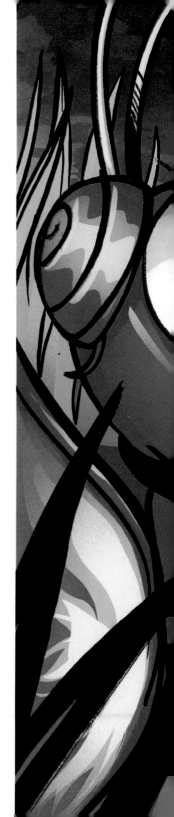

The three friends continued along, ignoring the zooming sounds of cars on the other side of the lawn. After about an hour, Laia noticed a strange kind of flower.

"Look over there," she said to her friends. "It's a scarlet petal, like the one on my wing. But it looks quite different surrounded by green. Is it a nettle or something I've never seen?"

The little red spot fluttered. Then, it puttered. And, finally, it sputtered. "I'm sorry I gave you a fright, but it's difficult for me to stay out of sight."

"You look like a ladybug," Lee, the grasshopper, said. "But where are your spots? Why are you all red?"

"My name is Dot," the ladybug did groan. Then she spread her oval wings. "But I haven't a single spot. Not even one!"

"We are looking for a fourth friend to join our merry crew," Laia chimed. "If you join us, instead of three, we can be two and two!"

 Dot squeaked, "Then that's just what I'll do!"

Laia flittered above her true friends and beamed a grin of glee. "This quest of mine was a difficult voyage, but here you all are – all three! A bee with no sting, a grasshopper with no song, and a ladybug with no spot—let me be honest, I like you a lot."

The three friends nodded their approval. "We like you too!" they all agreed. "A Butterfly Princess with a scarlet splash on her wing!"

Now, the clouds were coming out and the day was getting late. Laia knew that she had to head home. There was no time to wait. "Will you all return to the meadow with me? My mother would like to make us her honeyed hibiscus tea."

"But, how will we make it?" Dot, the ladybug, peeped. "Those growling beasts are so speedy. What if they never quit?"

Laia thought silently, wondering how they would solve their perilous plight. As she stood thinking, she saw a sudden streak of glittering light.

Sunrays began touching the earth, like fingers poking through the cloudy billows. She saw flashes of light shining here and there and beyond the road lined with willows.

"Are you speaking to me, Sun?" Laia asked, looking up to the sky. "Have you found a path through the cars' wrath, so we don't get hurt as they're zipping by?"

Laia realized that the nimble lights were the key. "Come on, my true friends! Stay close and follow me!"

Laia flew to the first sunlit flash filled with a courage that dispersed all fear. Ben buzzed, Lee hopped, and Dot fluttered always staying quite near. Once they were all grouped on a gleaming spot, Laia looked for the next shine from the sun, declaring their next stop.

First, they started on the grassy edge, and then they found themselves on the cement's ledge. They jumped from light to light like lilies atop an asphalt river. The cars flowed by causing the air around them to quiver. But not one of them was affected—not one did shiver.

The four friends hop-scotched across the street following each glimmer that did appear. They stayed safe as long as they were on the light's trail. When they arrived at the other end, they shouted a great cheer. They had made it past the roaring cars to the grassy vale!

"We did it! We made it to the other side!" Laia cried. "We won the race against those scary creatures, following the light as our guide!"

Lee hopped a leap, and Dot fluttered a loop. Ben buzzed a sweep, and Laia flew a swoop. How happy and clever they were together; and best of all, they were friends forever! Four friends true and true, not one or three, but two and two!

A bee with no sting.
A grasshopper with no song.
A ladybug with no spot.
And a butterfly who wanted to belong.

Laia gathered her true friends and led them back home to her tree. King Papa welcomed them warmly, and Queen Mama made them honeyed hibiscus tea.

Laia's quest had brought her those she loved best. Her life was full, but she couldn't wait to experience the rest.

This story is dedicated to all who have been beautifully marked by birth or life.

Go discover diverse friends in unlikely places!